Goyangi Means Cat

Christine McDonnell

PICTURES BY

Steve Johnson & Lou Fancher

VIKING

An Imprint of Penguin Group (USA) Inc.

For all children who have made the journey to a new home

—C.M.

For Nicholas

—S.J. & L.F.

The art was created in paper collage and acrylic and oil paint. The patterns used in the paper collage were selected to reflect the Eastern and Western worlds of Soo Min, the child in the story. The Korean words were drawn from the text: *family*, *home*, *mommy*, *daddy*, *child*, *safe*, *love*, and, expectedly, *cat*.

VIKING
Published by Penguin Group
Penguin Young Readers Group, 345 Hudson Street, New York, New York 10014, U.S.A.
Penguin Group (Canada), 90 Eglinton Avenue East, Suite 700, Toronto, Ontario, Canada M4P 2Y3
(a division of Pearson Penguin Canada Inc.)
Penguin Books Ltd, 80 Strand, London WC2R 0RL, England
Penguin Ireland, 25 St Stephen's Green, Dublin 2, Ireland (a division of Penguin Books Ltd)
Penguin Group (Australia), 250 Camberwell Road, Camberwell, Victoria 3124, Australia
(a division of Pearson Australia Group Pty Ltd)
Penguin Books India Pvt Ltd, 11 Community Centre, Panchsheel Park, New Delhi – 110 017, India
Penguin Group (NZ), 67 Apollo Drive, Rosedale, North Shore 0632, New Zealand
(a division of Pearson New Zealand Ltd)
Penguin Books (South Africa) (Pty) Ltd, 24 Sturdee Avenue, Rosebank, Johannesburg 2196, South Africa

First published in 2011 by Viking, a division of Penguin Young Readers Group

10 9 8 7 6 5 4 3 2 1

LIBRARY OF CONGRESS CATALOGING-IN-PUBLICATION DATA
McDonnell, Christine.
Goyangi means cat / by Christine McDonnell ; illustrated by Steve Johnson and Lou Fancher. — 1st ed.
p. cm.
ISBN 978-0-670-01179-7 (hardcover)
[1. Home—Fiction. 2. Korean Americans—Fiction. 3. Intercountry adoption—Fiction. 4. Adoption—Fiction. 5. Cats—Fiction.] I. Johnson, Steve, 1960– ill. II. Fancher, Lou, ill. III. Title.
PZ7.M47843Go 2011
[E]—dc22
2010043325

Manufactured in China

Goyangi Means Cat

WELCOME
HOME,
SOO!
엄마
아빠

어린이

When Soo Min came from Korea to her new home in America, she spoke no English. Her new family knew just a few Korean words.

Mok-da — eat

Chim-dae — bed

Bahp — rice

Jip — house

집 집
집 집 집
고양이
찝 집
사랑

In the first few days, Soo Min quickly taught them more words:

Anyah — no! when she didn't want to go to bed.

Ah-po — hurt, when she scraped her knee.

Gom — teddy bear, which she carried in the hood of her jacket.

Po-po — kiss, a gift she gave her parents.

She called the woman ***Omah*** and the man ***Apah***.

Best of all was ***Goyangi*** — the cat.

The woman's light eyes and the man's beard
were strange to Soo Min.
All the food was new except for baph.
But Soo Min loved Goyangi right from the start.
She followed the cat from room to room
playing hide and seek.

집먹다 고양이가
고양이키스고양
먹다 집쌀고
쌀집집
고양이먹다

침대 침대
고양이 고양이

At night Goyangi curled up on Soo Min's bed.
When she was frightened by a siren in the street,
she stroked Goyangi's soft fur.
When Soo Min missed her Korean friends,
Goyangi licked her hand with his towelly tongue.

In that first week, Soo Min went out
with her new parents to the park

and in the car

and to the library.

고양이
고양이
고양이

When she wanted to go back to the house,
she tugged on Omah's sleeve. She meant, "Let's go."
Omah didn't come, so Soo Min said, "*Goyangi*."
When Omah still didn't understand,
Soo Min said, "*Goyangi jip*."
She meant, "The cat is at the house. Let's go."
Soo Min said, "*Goyangi jip mok-da*."
She meant, "The cat is at the house and needs his food.
Let's go!"
She tugged on Omah's sleeve until they headed back.

One morning at the end of Soo Min's first week in her new house, when Apah was leaving, Goyangi slipped out the door, ran down the steps, and disappeared.

Soo Min noticed at breakfast.

"*Goyangi?*" she asked. Omah pointed to the door.

"*Goyangi jip?*" Soo Min asked.

Omah shook her head no and pointed. "Goyangi outside."

고양이

Soo Min didn't finish her breakfast. She sat by the window and watched the street.

"Let's go look for Goyangi," Omah said.

Soo Min and Omah walked up and down the block.

"*Goyangi*," Soo Min called. "*Goyangi*."

"Here, kitty kitty," Omah called. "Come home, Goyangi. Come home."

엄마
엄마
가족
고양이

Soo Min knew the cat was frightened
and wanted to come back to her.
She knew he was lonely and afraid.
Soo Min and Omah walked slowly
down the street.
Omah called, "Goyangi, come home.
Come home, kitty."

Back at the house, sitting on Omah's lap,

Soo Min cried and cried.

She cried for Goyangi.

She cried for Korea.

So many tears.

Omah held her and rocked her.
When Soo Min fell asleep on the couch,
Omah covered her with a blanket.

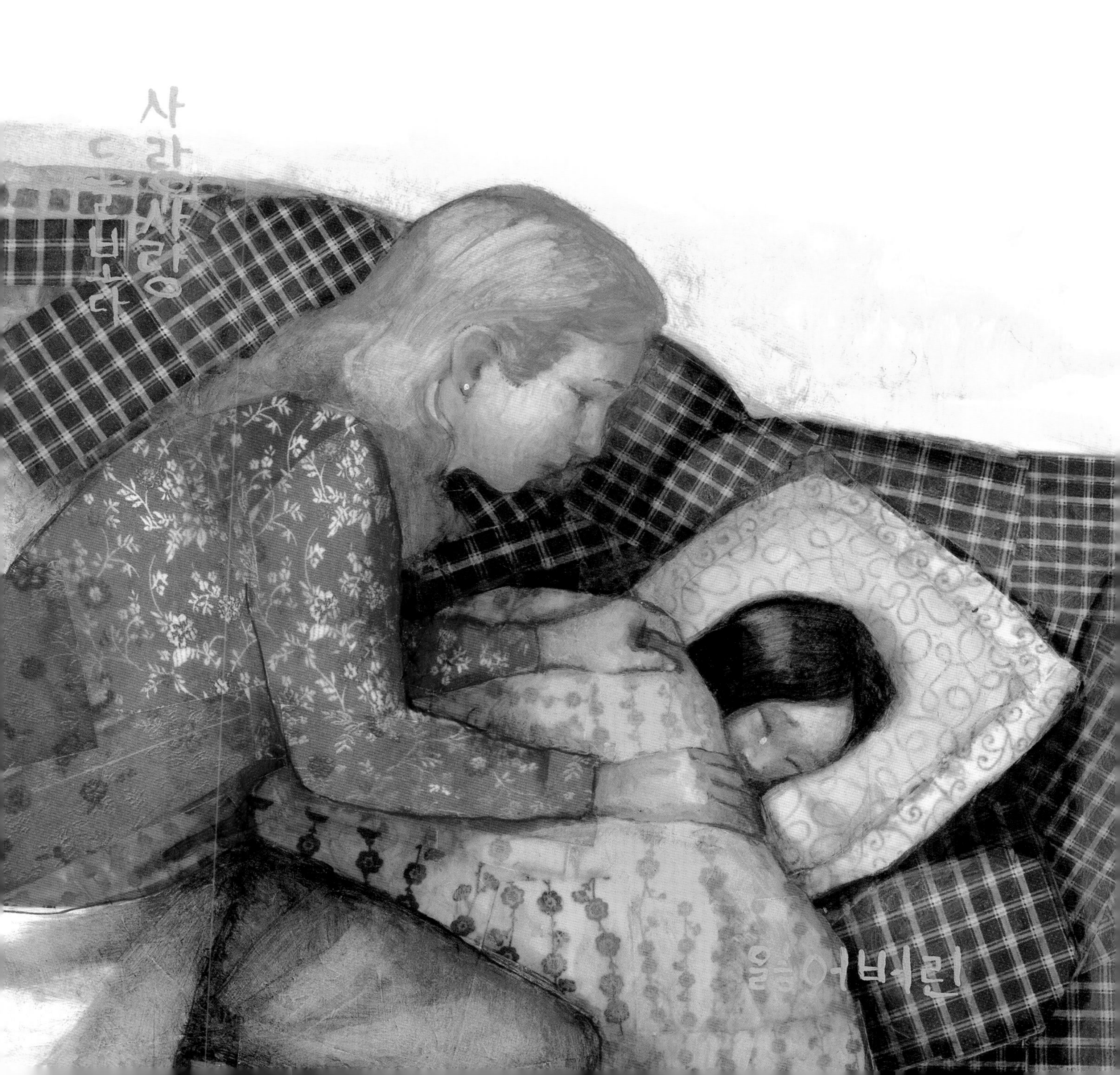

Soo Min slept until Apah returned from work.

She heard his footsteps in the hall.

Then Soo Min heard another sound.

She ran to the door.

"*Goyangi*," she said.

She knelt beside the cat and stroked his head.

He licked her hand and rubbed against her, purring loudly.

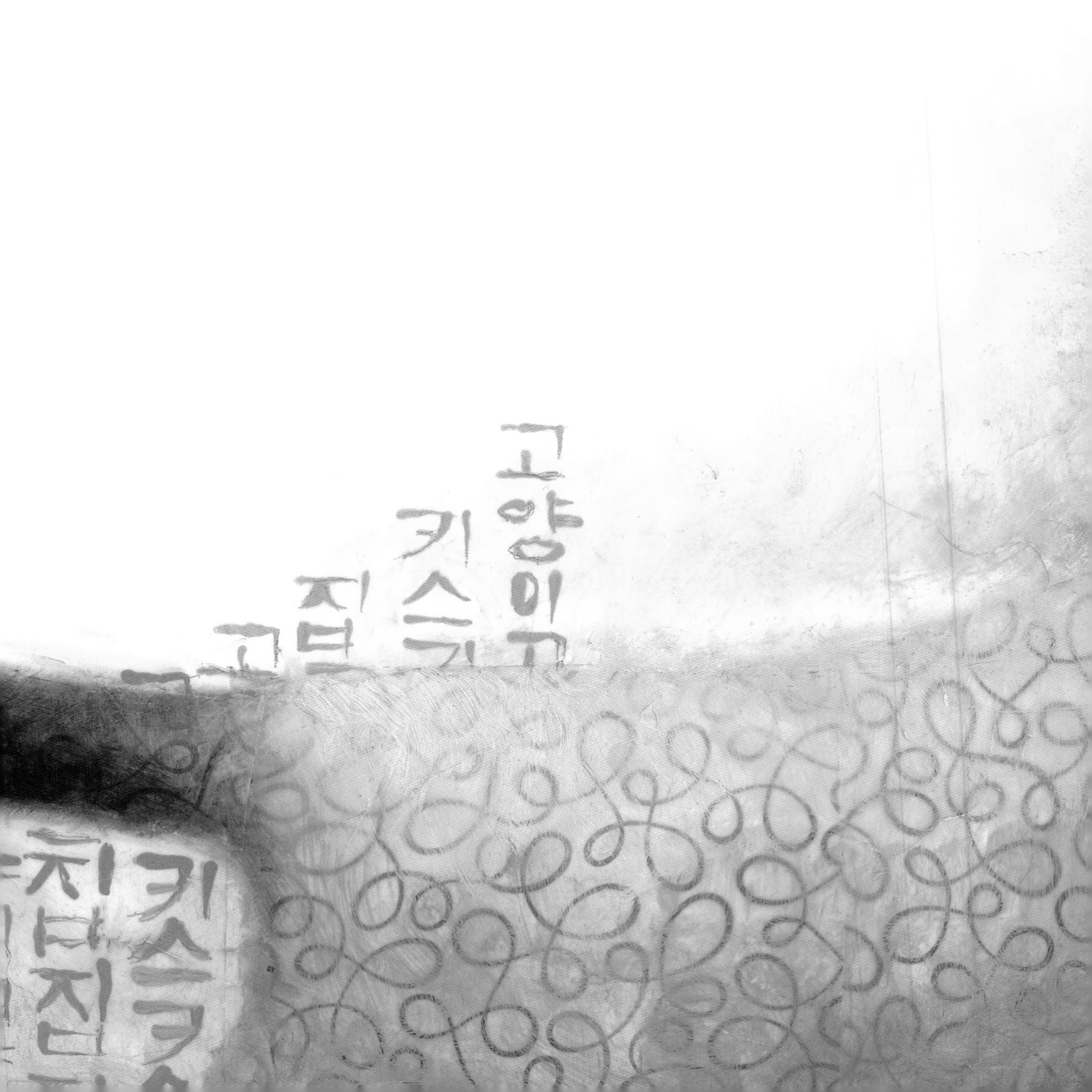

키스
고양이

"*Goyangi* home," Soo Min said. She smiled.